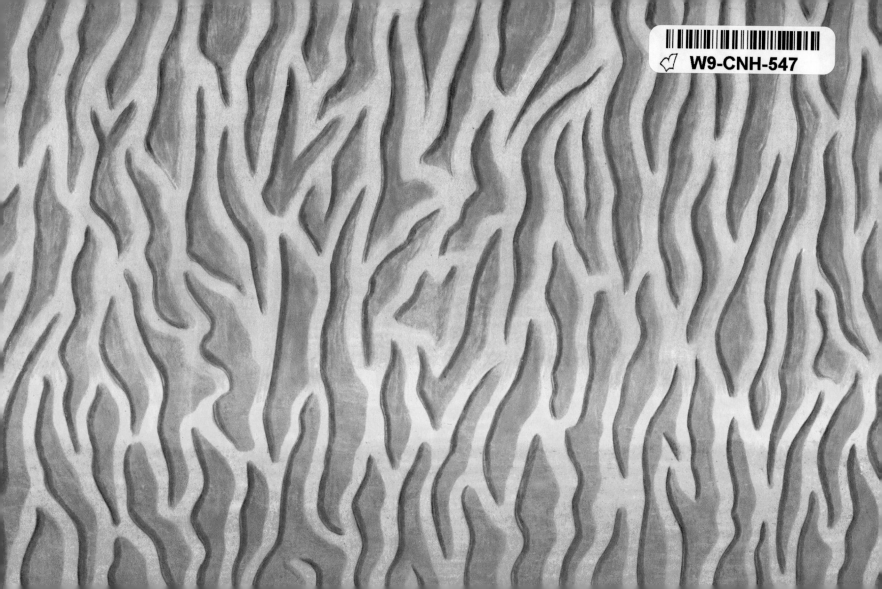

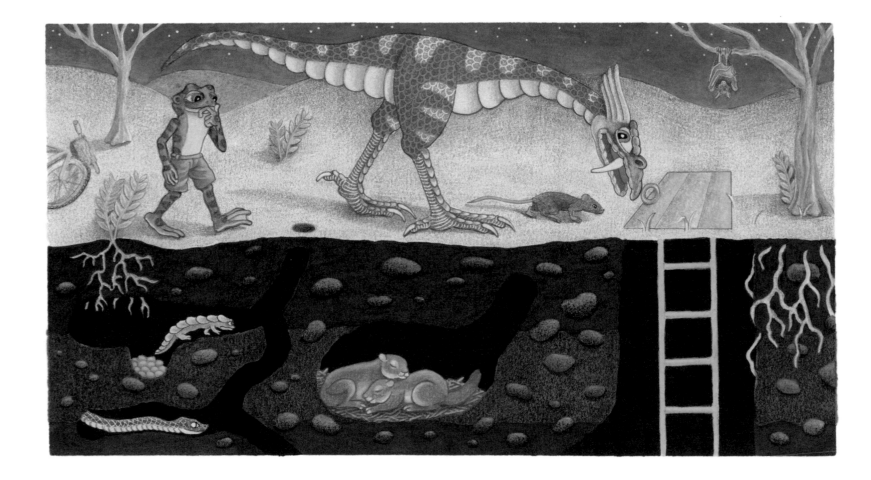

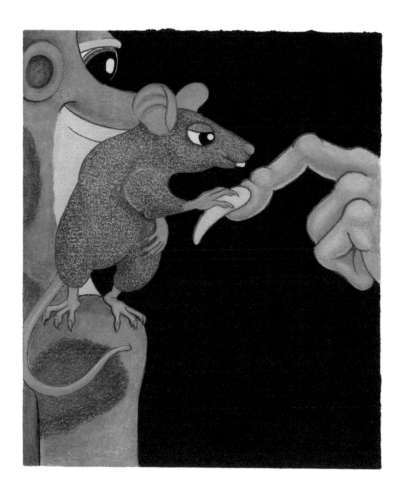

In memory of Wat
Thanks Aiyana, Fox, Mystery, Toki and Hoodrat.

McSWEENEY'S
McMULLENS

www.mcsweeneys.net

Copyright © 2012 Matt Furie

Matt Furie was born in Columbus, Ohio in 1979. This is his first book.

McSweeney's is a privately held company with wildly fluctuating resources.

All rights reserved, including the right of reproduction in whole or in part, in any form.

The McSweeney's McMullens will publish great new books — and new editions of out-of-print classics — for individuals and families of all kinds.

McSweeney's McMullens and colophon are copyright © 2012 McSweeney's & McMullens.

Printed in Singapore by Tien Wah Press

ISBN: 978-1-936365-56-2

First edition

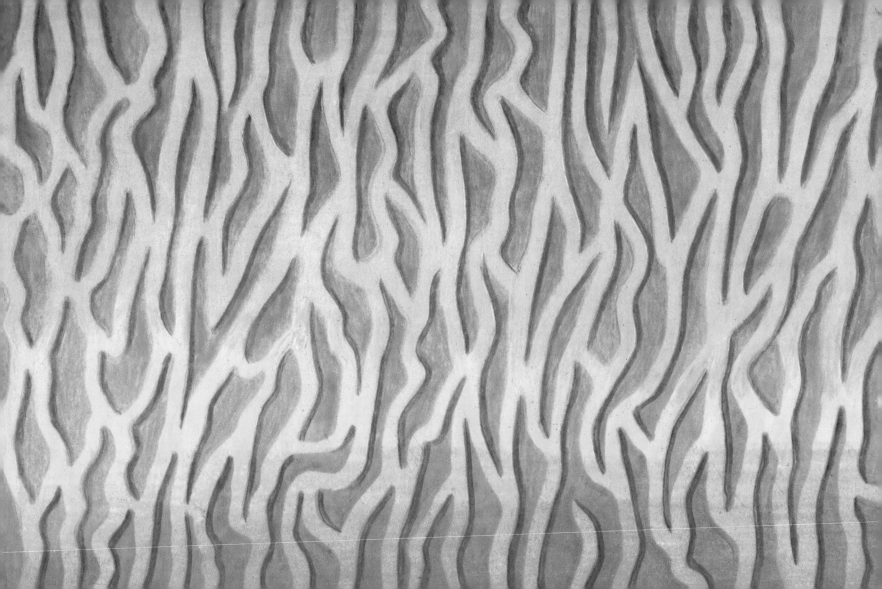